KAY THOMPSON'S ELOISE

# The Eloise Ready-to-Read Treasury

BASED ON THE ART OF HILARY KNIGHT

Ready-to-Read

**Aladdin**

NEW YORK · LONDON · TORONTO · SYDNEY

ALADDIN PAPERBACKS

An imprint of Simon & Schuster Children's Publishing Division

1230 Avenue of the Americas, New York, NY 10020

"Eloise" and related marks are trademarks of the Estate of Kay Thompson.

*Eloise and the Big Parade* text copyright © 2007 by the Estate of Kay Thompson

*Eloise and the Dinosaurs* text copyright © 2007 by the Estate of Kay Thompson

*Eloise and the Snowman* text copyright © 2006 by the Estate of Kay Thompson

*Eloise and the Very Secret Room* text copyright © 2006 by the Estate of Kay Thompson

*Eloise at the Wedding* text copyright © 2006 by the Estate of Kay Thompson

*Eloise Breaks Some Eggs* text copyright © 2005 by the Estate of Kay Thompson

*Eloise Has a Lesson* text copyright © 2005 by the Estate of Kay Thompson

*Eloise's New Bonnet* text copyright © 2007 by the Estate of Kay Thompson

These titles were previously published individually by Aladdin Paperbacks.

All rights reserved, including the right of reproduction in whole or in part in any form.

ALADDIN PAPERBACKS and related logo and READY-TO-READ are

registered trademarks of Simon & Schuster, Inc.

The text of this book was set in Century Old Style.

Printed and bound in the United States of America

0310 Lake Book Manufacturing, Melrose Park, IL

This Aladdin Paperbacks edition April 2009

Library of Congress Control Numbers:

*Eloise and the Big Parade* 2006933443 / *Eloise and the Dinosaurs* 2006012229

*Eloise and the Snowman* 2005030957 / *Eloise and the Very Secret Room* 2005029648

*Eloise at the Wedding* 2004016673 / *Eloise Breaks Some Eggs* 2004008891

*Eloise Has a Lesson* 2004009343 / *Eloise's New Bonnet* 2006012228

4 6 8 10 9 7 5 3

ISBN-13: 978-1-4169-9398-8

ISBN-10: 1-4169-9398-3

# KAY THOMPSON'S ELOISE

# Eloise and the Big Parade

STORY BY **Lisa McClatchy**

ILLUSTRATED BY **Tammie Lyon**

Ready-to-Read

**Aladdin**

NEW YORK · LONDON · TORONTO · SYDNEY

I am Eloise.
I live in The Plaza Hotel.

Today is the
Fourth of July parade.

Nanny loves a good parade.
So do I.

"Eloise," Nanny says,
"we must wear red, white,
and blue."

I wear a blue dress.
And white shoes.
And a red bow.

Nanny and I sit
right up front.

The marching band
arrives first.

I pretend I can play
the tuba.
Weenie plays the flute.

"Sit down, Eloise,"
Nanny says.

The clowns throw candy.
I grab as much as I can.

Then I try to juggle.
So does Weenie.

"Eloise! Sit down!"
Nanny yells.

The floats are next.
This one
is from New Orleans!
They throw party beads!

I wear as many as I can.
So does Weenie.
We dance in the street.

"Sit down, Eloise!"
Nanny yells.

Here come
the mounted police!

My favorite is
the palomino.
Nanny likes
the dapple gray.

I offer one some candy.
"No, no, no, Eloise!"
Nanny says.

A big car drives by us.
"There's the queen
of the parade!"
Nanny says.

I pretend I am a queen.
My bow is a crown.
My beads are jewels.
My dress is a gown.

Another car drives by.
I climb on up.

"Which queen are you?"
  the driver says.
"I am Queen of The Plaza!"
  I say.

Oh I love, love,
love parades!

# KAY THOMPSON'S ELOISE
# Eloise and the Dinosaurs

STORY BY **Lisa McClatchy**
ILLUSTRATED BY **Tammie Lyon**

**Aladdin Paperbacks**
NEW YORK · LONDON · TORONTO · SYDNEY

I am Eloise.
I am a city child.

I have a tutor.
His name is Philip.
He is boring, boring, boring.

Today
Philip is taking me
to the museum.

We are going
to see the dinosaurs.

Philip says,
"Here are the dinosaur halls!"

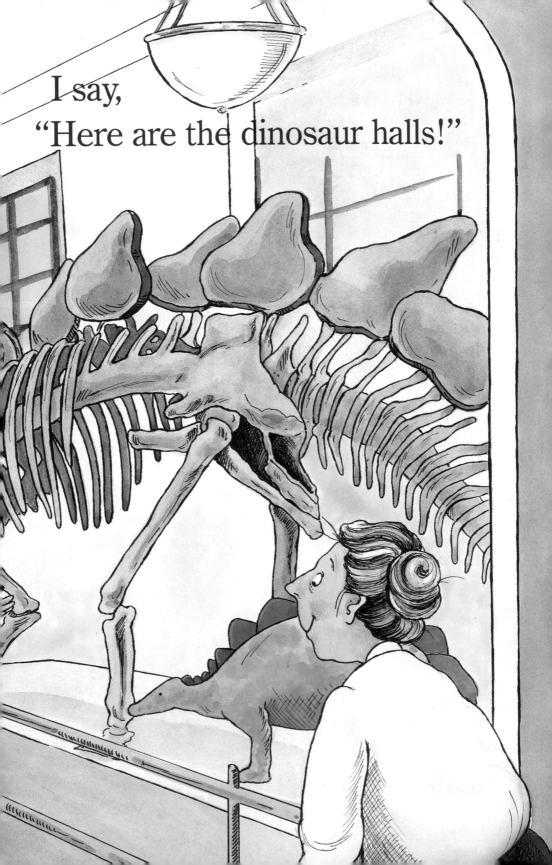

And he says,
"Please behave, Eloise."

And I say,
"Please behave, Eloise."

And he says,
"Here is a dinosaur."

Philip says,
"It is a Tyrannosaurus rex."

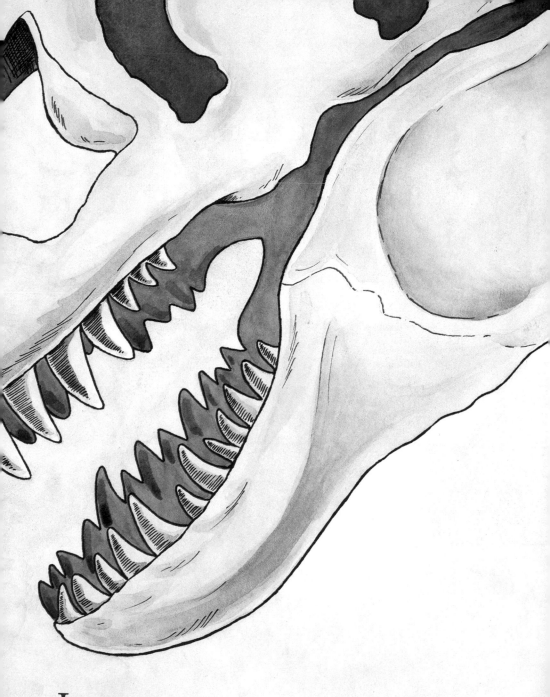

I say,
"It is a Tyrannosaurus rex."

Then he says,
"Please stop, Eloise."

Then I say,
"Please stop, Eloise."

And he says,
"Nanny, make her stop!"

Nanny says,
"No, no, no, Eloise!"

I skip over to
the triceratops.

My pink bow
looks just right
on his horn.

I cartwheel over to
the apatosaurus.

He needs a hat.

Philip says,
"Eloise, do not touch
the dinosaurs!"

Then Nanny says,
"Eloise,
leave the dinosaurs alone.
It is time for lunch."

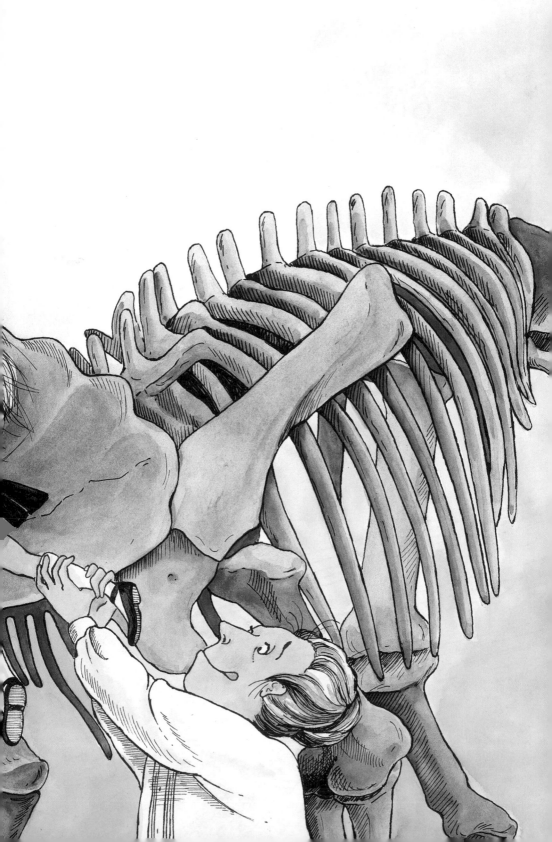

I say,
    "Good-bye, dinosaurs."

Oh I love, love, love
dinosaurs!

# KAY THOMPSON'S ELOISE

# Eloise and the Snowman

STORY BY **Lisa McClatchy**

ILLUSTRATED BY **Tammie Lyon**

Ready-to-Read
**Aladdin**
NEW YORK · LONDON · TORONTO · SYDNEY

I am Eloise.
I am six.
I live at The Plaza Hotel
on the tippy-top floor.

This is my room.
If I am very, very careful,
I can peek out my window.

It is snowing!

"Nanny," I say,
"we must go outside."
"Not now, Eloise,"
 Nanny says.
"It is time for breakfast."

"Breakfast can wait,"
I say.
Oh, I love, love,
love snow.

We cross the street
to Central Park.

I roll a ball of snow.
I roll another . . .
and another.

"Look, Nanny," I say.
"It is a snowman."

But something is missing.

I hail a driver
and his horse.
"To The Plaza at once,"
I say.

"Room service," I say,
"please bring me one carrot."

I race back to the snowman
and Nanny.

"Nanny," I say,
"do you like his nose?"
"Oh yes, dear," says Nanny.

But something is missing.

"Driver, away," I say.

Only the best tailors will do.
I get a hat, a coat,
a scarf, and gloves.

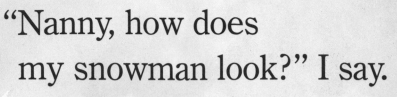
"Nanny, how does
my snowman look?" I say.

"Dashing, dear," says Nanny.
But something is missing.
"Back to The Plaza," I say.

"Eloise," says the manager.
"How may I help you?"

"We must build my snowman
    a house," I say.
"Send me
    your best carpenters."

"Eloise, dear, his house
is lovely," Nanny says.

But something is missing.

My breakfast.
"Nanny, let's go home,"
I say.

# Oh, I love, love, love snow.

# KAY THOMPSON'S ELOISE

# Eloise and the Very Secret Room

STORY BY **Ellen Weiss**

ILLUSTRATED BY **Tammie Lyon**

**Ready-to-Read**

**Aladdin**

NEW YORK · LONDON · TORONTO · SYDNEY

My name is Eloise.
I am six.

I live on
the tippy-top floor
of The Plaza Hotel.

But I can go all over.

This is Skipperdee.
He wears sneakers.
Sometimes.

Skipperdee and I
like to take walks.

Here is what I like to do:
go down
that very, very,
long, long hall.

(It is the one that
goes past the room
with the stringy mops.)

There is a room
that is so secret
only I know about it.

Skipperdee and I, anyway.

It says LOST AND FOUND.

Maybe it is lost,
but I found it.

There are very good things in it.

If you tie a lot of
ties together,
you can jump rope.

It is also a good room
to spin in.

If we get tired,
we take a nap on a
fur coat.

Here is what else I can do:
wear nineteen hats.

A tennis racket makes
a very good turtle carrier.

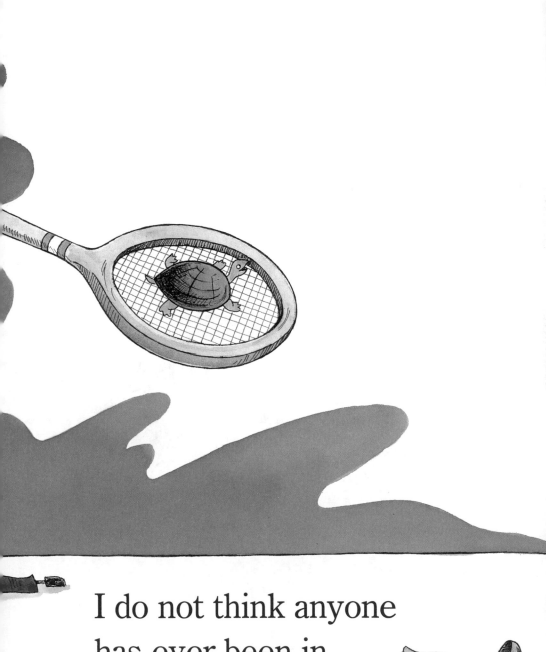

I do not think anyone
has ever been in
this room but me.

It is a good room
to practice hollering in.

# A hatbox makes a very good drum.

In comes Nanny.
"Eloise!" she says.
"Here you are!"

In comes the manager.
"Eloise!" he says.
"Here you are!"

"Of course I am here,"
I say.
"Where else would I be?"

"We found you
in the Lost and Found,"
says Nanny.

I was not lost at all.
I was right here
all the time.
Oooooooo I love, love, love
the Lost and Found.

Tomorrow I will see if that hat makes a good fishbowl.

# KAY THOMPSON'S ELOISE

# Eloise at the Wedding

STORY BY **Margaret McNamara**

ILLUSTRATED BY **Tammie Lyon**

**Aladdin Paperbacks**

NEW YORK · LONDON · TORONTO · SYDNEY

I am Eloise.
I live at The Plaza Hotel.

The Grand Ballroom
is busy today.

Cleaners are cleaning.

Cooks are cooking.

Waiters are waiting
for something to happen.

"What is going on?" I say.
"There will be
   a wedding today,"
Nanny says.

"I am going," I say.
I love, love, love weddings.

"You are not going,"
Nanny says.
"No one has asked you
to go."

That is true.
No one has asked me.

Not yet.

"It is time for your bath,"
Nanny says.

In the bath I am:
a sea captain,

a mermaid,

the Statue of Liberty.

After the bath
I am clean, clean, clean.

Nanny says,
"If you are very good
you may see the bride."

I am as good as I can be.

We peek inside
the Grand Ballroom.
There are men
who look like penguins.

There are ladies
with large hats.

Nanny says, "Oh dear, oh dear, oh dear."

I hear a noise.
It is a sad noise.
It is a crying noise.

It is coming from
the powder room.
I look inside.

There is the bride.
She is crying.

"Oh dear, oh dear,
oh dear," she says.
"What is wrong?" I say.

"The flower girl is sick,"
she says.
"How can I get married?"

"Do you want me to be
your flower girl?" I say.
"I do!" the bride says.

I am rather good
at being a flower girl.

Oooooooo I love,
love, love weddings.

# KAY THOMPSON'S ELOISE

# Eloise Breaks Some Eggs

STORY BY **Margaret McNamara**

ILLUSTRATED BY **Tammie Lyon**

**Aladdin Paperbacks**

NEW YORK · LONDON · TORONTO · SYDNEY

I am Eloise.
I am six.

I am a city child.
I live in a hotel
on the tippy-top floor.

This is Nanny.

She is my nanny.
My mother is mostly away.

"Eloise," says Nanny.
"It is time for your lesson."

I ask, "Piano?"
Nanny says, "No."

I ask, "French?"
Nanny says, "No."

I ask, "Poker?"
Nanny says, "No, no, no."

"It is time for
your cooking lesson.

# "Today you will cook eggs."

"I do not like to cook,"
I say.

"You like to break things,"
Nanny says.

"You break eggs
to cook them."

I say, "Let's go, go, go."

We take the elevator
to the kitchen.

I press every button.

"Today we will cook eggs,"
says the cook.

A bowl can make
a very good hat.
"No, no, no," says Nanny.

"Watch me," says the cook.
The cook is good.

"Now you try," he says.

"NO! NO! NO!" says Nanny.

"You broke the bowl!
You broke the plate!"
says the cook.

I say,
"I broke the eggs, too."

Nanny and
I take the elevator
to the tippy-top floor.
I press every button.

"You will never be a cook,"
says Nanny.
"How will you eat?"

I say, "Room service."
I pick up the phone.
I say, "It's me, Eloise.

"Two eggs,
and charge it, please.
Thank you very much."

KAY THOMPSON'S **ELOISE**

# Eloise Has a Lesson

STORY BY **Margaret McNamara**

ILLUSTRATED BY **Kathryn Mitter**

**Aladdin Paperbacks**

NEW YORK · LONDON · TORONTO · SYDNEY

I am Eloise.
I am six.

# I am a city child.

I live in a hotel
on the tippy-top floor.

This is Philip.

He is my tutor.
He is no fun.

Here is what I do not like:
doing math
for one half hour
in the morning.

Here is what I like:
teasing Philip.

# Philip says, "Hello, Eloise."

I say, "Hello, Eloise."

Philip says, "Math time."

I say, "Bath time?"

Philip says, "Eloise, please."

I say, "Eloise, please."

Philip says,
"What is five plus six?"

I say, "You do not know?"

"Nanny!" says Philip.
"Make Eloise behave."
"Eloise, behave," says Nanny.

Chalk makes a very good straw.

"What is five plus six?"
says Philip.

"Five plus six is the same as six plus five," I say.

Philip says, "Oh, Eloise."

I say, "Oh, Eloise."

Nanny says,
"Math time is nearly over.

"Time to finish up, up, up."

Philip says, "Eloise."

I say, "Philip."

Philip says, "Think."

I say, "I am thinking."

Philip says,
"What is five plus six?"

"It is eleven," I say.
"And the lesson is over."

Ooooooooo,
I absolutely love math.

# KAY THOMPSON'S ELOISE

# Eloise's New Bonnet

STORY BY **Lisa McClatchy**

ILLUSTRATED BY **Tammie Lyon**

**Aladdin Paperbacks**

NEW YORK · LONDON · TORONTO · SYDNEY

I am Eloise.
I am six.
I live in The Plaza hotel
on the tippy-top floor.

I have a dog.
His name is Weenie.

Here is what I like to do:
put sunglasses on Weenie.

Today the sun is shining.
Spring has sprung.
I put my sunglasses on too.

Nanny says, "Eloise,
you need a new hat."

Lampshades make
very good hats.

"No, no, no, Eloise,"
Nanny says.
"You need to find
a real hat."

"I know where to find
a real hat," I say.
"I will visit the kitchen."

Chef's hat makes
a very good hat.

"No, no, no, Eloise,"
Nanny says.
"That hat is too tall."

"I know," I say. "I
   will visit room service."

# Room service hats
# make very good hats.

"No, no, no, Eloise,"
Nanny says.
"That hat has no brim."

"Hmm," I say.
"I will visit
    the bell captain!"

Bell captain hats
make very good hats.

"No, no, no, Eloise," Nanny says. "We need a hat that is a pretty color."

I visit the lobby.
There are hats everywhere!

I try on a lady's hat.
It is a pretty color,
and it has a bird on top.
"Perfect," I say.

Nanny and the manager
do not agree.

"Please give the lady
her hat back,"
Nanny says.

"Sorry."

"Eloise, I have a surprise,"
Nanny says.
She hands me a box.

Inside is a new hat
just for me.

Oh, I love, love, love hats!